T0144020

Sunny Green's Adventures

S.J. HANSFORD

To order additional copies of this book, contact:
Xlibris
1-888-795-4274
www.Xlibris.com
Orders@Xlibris.com

ISBN: 978-1-7960-7654-7 (sc)
ISBN: 978-1-7960-7653-0 (e)

Print information available on the last page

Rev. date: 12/05/2019

Sunny Green's Adventures

S.J. Hansford

Hi my name is Sunny Green! It's a pleasure to meet you. Would you like to be my friend today?

I think I'll go find myself a new friend today.
I'll take a trip to New Jersey and look for my
new friend.

I should grab a bite to eat before I get on the airplane to fly to New Jersey.

Wow! Those meteors were delicious! I think I ate too many, now I have gas. I'm letting out a lot of steam! HAHAHAHA

Ok, now I am on my way to New Jersey. I see a kid all alone! I wonder why. Maybe he'll be my friend today. He's dressed differently than everyone else.

I think I may have landed on the wrong part of the earth today. Everyone is dressed so cool! I think I may have to try and blend in. What on earth should I wear?!

I think I'll start with the first store. There's a lot of cool clothes and even cooler looking people. WOW! I'm really feeling this fitted WHEELUP hat. It fits me nicely along with the clothing and my footwear.

Hey, I wonder why he's all alone saying to himself, "I'm tired of being picked on and bullied by a bunch of bullies". Hmmm, I never heard that word before. I wonder what it means!

Why are they saying he's "done up" and that his style is trash? That's weird! I always thought "trash" was garbage, and "done up" meant that you were tired of standing up! Why are these people so mean to him? They are saying he "doesn't want no sauce". I like sauce, especially on spaghetti.

UMMMMM YUMMY!!!!

I don't like the word "bully". I think I'll have to find a cool way to make everyone a "tully". It's a word that's used on my planet. It means:

True

Unconditional

Loyalty

Love

Yourselves

That's right! Sunny Green will make everyone "tullies" instead of "bullies". I like that!

Now, they are leaving him all alone. I think I'll speak to him, and try to become friends. "Hey, wazzup, sun. My name is Sunny Green. What's good with you?" He's not talking to me. I wonder why? He looks sad. Maybe he's upset.

I wonder if I can cheer him up somehow! What can I do to make him smile? "What's your name, bro?", I ask. He tells me to "step off!" I don't understand! What does he want me to step off of? There isn't any steps near us! That's weird. What can he be referring to?

I know what I can do! "Yo bro, step off with me! Let me show you something. Sunny Green keeps that green on deck at all times sun, that's my word!"

I take him inside the clothing store where I used my green bills to purchase my cool clothes. He's stepping with me now. "Bro, pick out whatever cool items you'd like. Everything's on me! I got you, sun!", I say trying to encourage him to have a good 'ol sunny time. He begins to smile a little. That's cool!

"You're looking hot now, sun!", I exclaimed. "HAHAHAHA!", he busted out in laughter. He called me sun, but my name is Sunny Green! Why would he call me sun? That's crazy weird.

Everyone likes him now, because his looks are on fleek and his confidence is all the way up! HAHAHAHA! I'll educate the bullies on how cool it is to become tullies. Maybe they'll get "tully" with it! HAHAHAHA! That's what I'll do; so, the bullied don't become bullies, and the bullies stop bullying and everyone becomes tullies. That's going to be so cool.

Now his swag is on level 10, all the way up! HAHAHAHA! That means cool, if you didn't know. Hey look! Here come the same guys that were picking on him. They're talking to him now, telling him his clothes are "lit" and on "fleek". Now their calling him a baller. He feels so confident about himself now. Why didn't anyone try and help build up his self-confidence and help him feel good about himself? This would have avoided the bullies picking on him. But all it took was Sunny Green's act of kindness to get the job done! My work here is finished!

I think it's time for me to get fly with it, and fly back into space! HAHAHA

Show small gestures of kindness to someone in need. It's the greatest recipe to brighten anyone's day!

Printed in the United States
By Bookmasters